My Granny Went to Market
Round-the-World Counting Rhyme

written by Stella Blackstone

illustrated by Christopher Corr

Barefoot Books

BROMLEY LIBRARIES

3 0128 70023 1791

D0244003

My granny went to market
to buy a flying carpet.

She bought the flying carpet
from a man in Istanbul.
It was trimmed with yellow tassels,
and made of knotted wool.

Next she went to Thailand
and flew down from the sky
to buy herself two temple cats,
Puyin and Puchai. *

*'Puyin' means little girl 'Puchai' means little boy

Then she headed westwards
to the land of Mexico;
she bought three fierce and funny masks,
one pink, one blue, one yellow.

The flying carpet seemed to know
exactly where to take her;
they went to China next,
to buy four lanterns made of paper.*

*the symbol on the lanterns means 'double happiness'

'To Switzerland!' cried Granny
as the carpet turned around.
She bought five cowbells there,
that made a funny clanking sound.

'Now Africa!' sang Granny,
'We must wake the morning sun!'
They spiralled south to Kenya
where she bought six booming drums.

Next they travelled northwards,
past the homes of mountain trolls,
to stop a while in Russia
for seven nesting dolls.

'Australia,' Granny ordered,
'Take me down to Alice Springs.
I want eight buzzing boomerangs
that fly back without wings.'

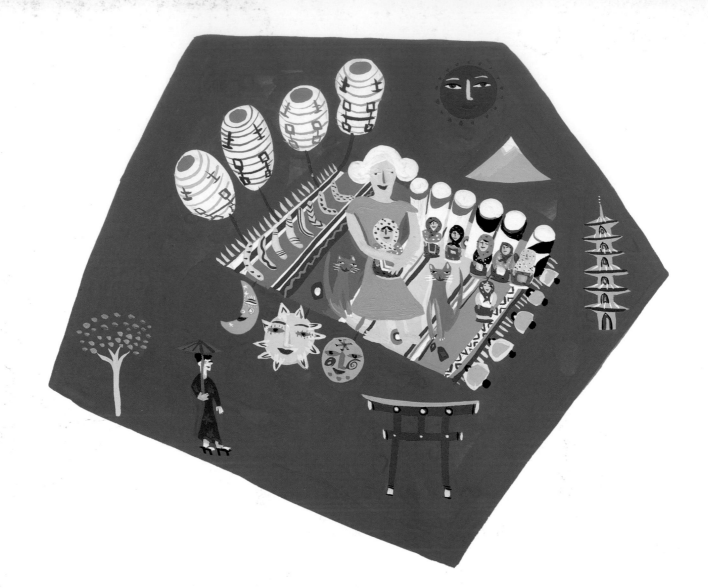

Then Granny sighed, 'I've bought so much,
but nothing Japanese!'
In Tokyo she found nine kites
that fluttered in the breeze.

But best of all, she met me
in the mountains of Peru,
where she gave me ten black llamas
and a magic carpet too!

And I flew away to ...

one carpet 1

two cats 2

three masks 3

four lanterns 4

five cowbells 5

six drums 6

seven nesting dolls 7

eight boomerangs 8

nine kites 9

ten llamas 10

For Felix — S. B.
For Eva Sugrue, my grandmother — C. C.

Barefoot Books
124 Walcot Street
Bath BA1 5BG

Text copyright © 1995 by Stella Blackstone
Illustrations copyright © 2005 by Christopher Corr
The moral right of Stella Blackstone to be identified as the author and
Christopher Corr to be identified as the illustrator of this work has been asserted

First published in Great Britain in 2005 by Barefoot Books Ltd
This paperback edition first published in 2006
All rights reserved. No part of this book may be reproduced in any form or by any means,
electronic or mechanical, including photocopying, recording or by any information
storage and retrieval system, without permission in writing from the publisher

This book was typeset in Kosmik
The illustrations were prepared in gouache on Fabriano paper

Graphic design by Louise Millar, London
Colour separation by Grafiscan, Verona
Printed and bound in China by Printplus Ltd

This book has been printed on 100% acid-free paper

Paperback ISBN 1-905236-38-7

British Cataloguing-in-Publication Data:
a catalogue record for this book is available from the British Library

798